WIZARD TALES

retold by
Corinne Denan

illustrated by
Lynn Sweat

Troll Associates

CONTENTS

The Sorcerer's Apprentice

Many, many years ago, there lived a strange and powerful Sorcerer. He was very tall and very bony, with a long nose that came to a point. He always dressed in wide, flowing gowns covered with mystical, magical stars. His wisps of hair were snowy white. And he was never seen in public without his tall, pointed cap.

In those days, there were plenty of plain old wizards about, but the Sorcerer was not one of them. Not at all! Other wizards would disappear in big clouds of smoke and then reappear seconds later at a different place. But not the Sorcerer. *He* traveled on horseback. He *could* have traveled by smoke puffs if he had wished, of course. But horseback, he felt, was more dignified, even if it was a good deal slower.

The Sorcerer lived in a huge stone castle that sat on top of a high hill. It stood all by itself, with no other dwellings in sight, for he did not like to be bothered by neighbors. Steep, winding stairs led down into the Sorcerer's dark cellar. It was there that he kept all his magic books, charms, powders, and special potions. These were closely guarded secrets, for they would be dangerous if they fell into the wrong hands. After all, these were the things that had made the Sorcerer as great as he was. And he intended to keep it that way.

Except for the Sorcerer himself, only one person was allowed in the cellar. This was Raymond, the Sorcerer's apprentice. Raymond was a young boy who wanted to learn how to become a sorcerer. So, in return for doing chores around the cellar, the Sorcerer taught Raymond some of the simple secrets of sorcery. However, there were problems. For Raymond was not a very hard worker. As a matter of fact, he was rather lazy. If a job could be bungled in some way, Raymond would find the way! It was only because Raymond was a likable lad that the Sorcerer kept him around at all.

Now, in the corner of the Sorcerer's cellar stood a huge wooden tub. One of Raymond's jobs was to keep this tub filled with water. Of all his chores, Raymond hated this one the most. For it meant that he had to go up and down the steep, winding stairs with heavy buckets, over and over again. How he wished someone would do the work for him!

Whenever the Sorcerer was about to perform a complicated spell, he would close and lock the cellar door. Raymond would have to remain upstairs and amuse himself in other ways.

One afternoon, the Sorcerer was so busy with a very difficult spell that he forgot to shut the cellar door. Raymond, being naturally curious about the mysterious ways of sorcery, decided to sit quietly at the top of the stairs and see what he could learn.

The Sorcerer went from shelf to shelf gathering brightly colored powders, dried bats' wings, and dragons' teeth. Soon he had both hands full. He was about to dump all the ingredients into a big cauldron, when he noticed that he had left it in the far corner of the cellar. Rather than call for Raymond, he decided to take care of it himself. He walked a few feet to a wooden broom leaning against the wall. Then he walked around in a circle four times. He jumped up and down twice, and then chanted:

Zippity, zappity, zidderly zee.
Broom, bring back my cauldron to me.

Raymond's eyes grew wide with wonder. For, as he watched, two spindly arms sprouted from

the broom—and the straw parted and became feet! The broom walked over to the cauldron, picked it up, and set it down right in front of the Sorcerer.

Raymond could hardly believe his eyes and ears! Now he knew one of the Sorcerer's spells. He quickly ran from the top of the steps so that the Sorcerer would not discover him there.

His work would become a lot easier, Raymond thought. The next time the Sorcerer went away for a day and left him with the chores, Raymond would know just what to do. He could hardly wait!

But Raymond had to wait a very long time, for the Sorcerer was hard at work and did not leave the castle. After a while, Raymond forgot about the magic spell.

Then one day, the Sorcerer announced that he was to be the guest of honor at the Sorcerers' Convention. He would leave the next morning and be gone the entire day.

"While I am gone, Raymond," he said, "you are to clean the cellar floor, wash out the cauldron, and fill the water tub right up to the top. I have been working hard, and the cellar is a mess. I want it clean and sparkling when I return."

When Raymond awoke the following morning, the Sorcerer had already gone. Raymond had a lot to do. He set about doing the easy tasks first. When everything was clean and in order, Raymond was already exhausted. And he still had that huge water tub to fill. He leaned back against the wall and groaned.

Then his eyes fell upon the broom standing in the corner. And he remembered the wonderful spell he had seen the Sorcerer perform.

"I have worked hard," he said to himself. "Now is the perfect time to try out the Sorcerer's spell."

So Raymond stood before the broom and did just what the Sorcerer had done. He walked around in a circle four times, and jumped up and down twice. Then he chanted:

Zippity, zappity, zidderly zee.
Broom, fetch my bucket—
Bring water for me.

He held his breath a few moments, almost afraid to see what would happen. Then, sure enough, thin wooden arms and straw feet appeared. The broom walked over to the bucket, picked it up, and began to climb the steep stairs.

A few minutes later, the broom returned with

a bucketful of water, dumped it into the tub, and went back for more. Raymond sat down and watched his work being done for him. He was very proud of himself!

Up and down, back and forth went the broom, again and again. Soon the water tub was filled almost to the brim. Raymond figured that the broom would know enough to stop when the water reached the very top.

But the broom kept bringing more and more buckets of water. In no time at all, the water in the tub had overflowed and began to spill out onto the cellar floor. The Sorcerer's magic powders and books were getting wet. The Sorcerer would be furious!

"I must do something to stop the broom!" Raymond cried.

Then it occurred to him to try the same spell he had used before, but this time in reverse. So the next time the broom came down the stairs, Raymond walked around in a circle four times, jumped up and down twice, and chanted:

Zippity, zappity, zidderly zee.
Broom, stop bringing water to me.

But the broom kept right on marching.

Raymond tried saying other magical words, but nothing worked. The water was already up to his knees. He was becoming desperate. He had to stop that broom! Oh, what could he do?

Then he had an idea. He picked up the Sorcerer's ax, and waited. When the broom came down the stairs, Raymond swung the ax, and cut the broom into three pieces.

"That will stop you!" Raymond cried.

But, to his amazement, the *pieces* kept right on marching! They grew arms and feet, and they picked up two other buckets. Now there were three of them! They began to move faster and faster. Three times as much water poured in.

Everything in the cellar began to bob up and down. The water continued to rise higher and higher, swirling round and round. Raymond decided to head for the stairs while he could still walk. But suddenly, the wooden stairs went floating past him!

Poor Raymond thought, "This will be the end of me. I will surely drown before the Sorcerer gets back."

Just as Raymond was about to disappear under the rushing water, the Sorcerer appeared at the cellar door.

"What have you done?" he cried.

"Oh, Sorcerer, help me," cried Raymond. "I tried to use one of your magic spells, and now everything has gone wrong."

"You simpleton!" roared the Sorcerer. "I warned you about this. I should let you drown!"

But the Sorcerer really did have a kind heart. He lifted his arms and uttered some strange-sounding words. Within seconds, the water disappeared. Everything returned to its proper place. Even the broom stood quietly in its corner. Poor Raymond staggered to the stairs and sat there gasping for air.

The Sorcerer was furious. "You will never make a good sorcerer," he said. "You are nothing but a fool, and I will not have a fool for my apprentice."

Before Raymond knew what was happening, the Sorcerer gave him a swift kick that sent him flying head over heels through the air. He landed upside-down in his bed at home—but oh, it felt good to be there!

The Sorcerer never saw his apprentice again. And Raymond never saw the Sorcerer again. And, as far as we know, both were just as glad.

The Magic Crystal Ball

Once upon a time, there was a King who decided to build a magnificent estate in the country. So he told his foresters to go into the woods and begin clearing the land. The King's three sons went out with the foresters every day to watch them chop down the trees.

The King did not know that a wicked witch lived in those woods. And when she saw her trees being chopped down, she was enraged. She vowed to get even with the King.

One day, only two of the King's sons went to watch the foresters at work. Quickly, the witch changed one of the sons into an eagle and the other son into a whale.

When the King heard what had happened, he was overcome with grief. But his third son, the youngest, said, "Don't weep, Father. I will seek out the Great Wizard who lives in the hills. Perhaps he can restore my brothers to their human shapes."

The King had very little faith in his youngest son. But he let him go.

For months, the Prince wandered about in

search of the Wizard. Soon he came to a land where everything was bathed in a yellow light. And he saw an old man sitting under a tree.

"What land is this?" asked the Prince.

"You are in the land of the Golden Sun," said the old man.

"I am looking for the Great Wizard," said the Prince. "Does he live here?"

"Well, we do have a Wizard," said the old man, "but I cannot say if he is great or not. He is certainly wicked and spiteful. Right now he is holding captive a lovely Princess—the only child of our King."

"Show me where she is held," said the young Prince, "and I will rescue her."

The old man smiled and said, "Many have already tried and all have failed. But, if you wish to go, I will tell you how to get to the Wizard's castle."

At once the Prince set off toward the Wizard's castle. Before long he came upon two giants engaged in a great fight. They were grunting and bellowing and flinging one another upon the ground.

The Prince cried out, "Stop your fighting! That is a silly way to settle an argument!"

The giants looked at the Prince in surprise. "You had better get out of the way, little one," said one of the giants.

"First, tell me what you are fighting about," replied the Prince. He sounded far braver than he felt.

The other giant pointed to an old cap on the ground. "The winner of the fight gets the cap," he said.

"But that's only an old cap," said the Prince. "Why fight over it?"

"Because it is a magic cap, that's why," puffed the first giant. "Whoever puts that cap on his head can wish himself wherever he wants to go."

"Well, that's a different matter, of course," said the Prince. "Still, fighting does seem a silly way to spend one's time. I have an idea. I shall take the cap over to that tree. Then the two of you will race for it. Whoever reaches the cap first gets to keep it."

The giants looked at each other. They were both out of breath and did not want to fight any longer. This seemed like a sensible idea. So they agreed.

The Prince put the cap on his head and walked toward the tree. "This is an interesting adventure," he said to himself, "but it is not helping me to rescue the Princess. How I wish I were at the Wizard's castle right now."

And puff! In a flash, the Prince found himself standing right in front of a gloomy, gray castle. "Of course!" he said. "The cap brought me here! Those giants must be dreadfully angry. But I will return the cap after I rescue the Princess."

The Prince drew his sword and entered the castle. He was ready to fight anyone who got in his way.

But, to his surprise, he met no one at all. The castle seemed to be empty. At last, at the end of a long, dark passageway, he saw a small door. He pushed it open and stepped inside. There before him was the ugliest old woman he had ever seen. She was wrinkled and bent, and her hair hung to the floor in stringy gray tangles.

"I seem to be in the wrong place," said the Prince. "You can't possibly be the Princess." And he turned to leave, because the old woman was too ugly to look at.

"Wait," the old woman cried in a raspy voice. "Before you go, look into this mirror." And she held a small looking glass beside her face. The Prince looked into the mirror and gasped. In the

glass he saw the loveliest Princess he had ever seen. She had smooth, shining hair, large green eyes, and a beautiful smile. The Prince fell in love with her, and could not take his eyes away from the looking glass.

"That is my face," said the old woman in her croaking voice. "The Wizard has put me under a spell. He lives in the tower of this dreadful castle. I am doomed to be an ugly old woman until someone has the courage to break the spell."

"I'm not known for my courage," said the Prince, keeping his eyes on the lovely face in the looking glass. "But I promise that I will try."

"Others have tried and failed," said the old woman. "To break the spell, you must hold in your hands a certain crystal ball. To get this crystal ball, you must fight and kill the mighty bull that waits outside the castle."

"Oh, dear," murmured the Prince. "I'm not at all sure I know how to do that."

"It will try to pierce you with its horns," said the old woman, "but you will kill it if you drive your sword straight through its heart. When the bull is dead, a great bird will spring from its body. The bird will hold a fire-hot egg in its claws. You must seize the egg before the bird flies away. Inside the egg is the crystal ball. When you hold it in your hands, the Wizard must obey your every command."

Then the young Prince drew his sword and left the castle. Just outside the castle walls stood the ferocious bull. The huge beast lowered its head and began to charge. The Prince grew pale with fear.

Again and again, the bull's powerful horns ripped at the Prince and tossed him into the air. Time and again, the Prince thought the end had come. But he had promised to try, and try he did. Suddenly, he saw his chance. Gathering all his strength, the Prince thrust his sword at the heart of the bull. With a mighty groan, the monster fell to the ground.

At once, a giant bird rose from the bull's body. And in its claws was a fiery egg. But before the Prince could seize the egg, the bird flew high into the sky.

"Oh, I have failed," cried the Prince. "The crystal ball is inside the egg, and now I shall never get it!"

Just then, the Prince heard a mighty swoosh of wings. He raised his eyes and saw a great eagle swoop down upon the giant bird. And the Prince knew that the eagle was his brother.

The two birds fought fiercely in the sky. But when the eagle tore at the other bird's claws, the fiery egg began to fall. Alas—it fell into the rolling sea.

"Oh, no, dear brother," cried the Prince. "Now surely all is lost!" And once more he was filled with despair.

Suddenly the Prince heard the sound of great waves in the ocean. An enormous whale was swimming toward shore and spouting water as it swam. Balanced on the top of the waterspout was the very egg that had fallen into the sea. With a toss of its great head, the whale threw the egg onto the shore.

"Oh, my brother," cried the Prince, "you have saved us all!"

The Prince ran to the egg, and cracked it open. Then he seized the crystal ball, returned to the castle, and ran up the narrow, winding stairs. At the top of the castle tower, he flung open the door. And there sat the Wizard.

The Wizard was old and wrinkled. His fingers were long and bony, and his hair flowed about his head like writhing snakes. Upon his shoulder sat a great, speckled bird.

As the Prince entered the tower, the Wizard said, "Your power is even greater than mine. So I must do your bidding." And the Wizard bowed low before the young Prince.

"Very well," said the Prince. Then he held up the crystal ball and said, "Restore my two brothers to their human shapes."

"It is done," answered the Wizard.

Once more the Prince looked into the crystal ball. And there stood the same beautiful Princess he had seen in the looking glass. The Prince's heart grew full as he saw her smile.

Then the Prince turned to the evil Wizard, and said, "You have led a wicked life, so you must be banished from this land. Begone!"

And puff! The Wizard disappeared in a cloud of gray dust.

Then, still holding the crystal ball, the Prince ran to the room where he had last seen the ugly old woman. And there stood the beautiful Princess.

"You are the bravest of all," said the Princess.

The Prince smiled and said, "I wish that you would be my wife and come with me to my land."

The Princess held out her hand. "That is my wish, too," she said.

The Prince and the Princess were very happy together. And in time, a lovely baby girl was born to them. When the little girl grew older, the

Prince told her this tale, and she asked, "But Father, did you ever return the magic cap to the giants?"

Then the Prince handed her the crystal ball. When she looked into it, she saw the magic cap, hanging from the branch of a tree. Next to the tree were the two giants. And they were still fighting.

"Look, Father," said the little Princess. "Some things never seem to change!"

And the Prince smiled at his daughter's wisdom.

The Wizard's Spell

Once upon a time there lived a handsome and gentle King named Harold. He ruled wisely and well, despite the fact that he was very young. If he had one fault, as far as his subjects were concerned, it was that he was not married. And his subjects wished to have a Queen of the realm. Time after time, young women had been introduced to the King, but Harold showed no interest in any of them.

Now, on one side of the King's realm lived an evil Wizard, who had a very ugly daughter named Esmerelda. On the other side of the King's realm was the kingdom of the Swan Fairy. She had a beautiful young daughter named Princess Helena. The Swan Fairy knew of Harold's kindness and wisdom, and she felt that he would make a perfect husband for her lovely daughter. So, one day she sent an ambassador to see the King.

After the ambassador was shown into the royal throne room, he cleverly brought the conversation around to the beautiful Princess Helena.

"I have brought you a picture of the Princess," said the ambassador.

The young King was overwhelmed by the Princess in the picture. Try as he might, he could not stop thinking of her. This had never happened to him before. The following morning, he called his servants and told them to prepare for a journey to the palace of the Swan Fairy. He had decided to ask for Helena's hand in marriage. His entire kingdom was overjoyed at the news.

The news also reached the Wizard's kingdom. And the Wizard's daughter, Esmerelda, was very unhappy. Not wishing to see his daughter unhappy, the Wizard decided to stop the King's marriage. He immediately sent for his old servant, Rupert.

Then, chanting some magical words, the Wizard used his great and evil powers to make Rupert and King Harold change places. In a flash, Rupert took on the appearance of the handsome King and continued the journey to the palace of the Swan Fairy. The real King Harold was whisked away and imprisoned in the Wizard's dark tower. There he would stay until he was presented to Esmerelda.

Accompanied by the King's servants, the false King arrived at the Swan Fairy's palace. He was greeted by the Swan Fairy and her daughter.

They did not know he was really a servant. Much to the Swan Fairy's surprise, the false King spoke rudely and had no manners. In fact, he did not even recognize Helena as his bride-to-be.

"You have had her picture for two weeks now," said the Swan Fairy. "How is it that you do not recognize my daughter?"

"I can't recall ever seeing her picture," replied Rupert truthfully. Then he added, "It has been a long, boring trip, and I am very tired." And with that, he went off to the first empty room he could find. He lay down and was soon snoring so loudly that he could be heard at the other end of the kingdom.

The Swan Fairy was shocked. This could not be the gentle, refined Harold. Helena was dreadfully hurt by Rupert's manner. She ran into her mother's arms and sobbed, "The King I have heard about has a kind heart. This man does not. And he is so rude. How can I possibly marry him?"

Just then, there was a knock at the door, and the servant of the real King Harold entered. He told the Swan Fairy that he believed his master was under an evil spell.

"He does not act at all like himself," said the

servant. "In fact, he started acting strangely during the journey. I fear some Wizard has cast a spell on him."

The Swan Fairy thought for a while, and then went to her secret chamber. She opened a trunk and took from it a magic looking glass. The looking glass would show her anything she wanted to see. And right now, she wanted to see the real King Harold, wherever he might be.

Lo and behold! When she looked in the glass, she saw Harold, imprisoned in the Wizard's tower. There he sat, gazing sadly at Helena's picture. Now the Swan Fairy wondered who the false King was. When she looked in the mirror it revealed the truth. She saw the reflection of the Wizard's horrid servant.

The Swan Fairy told her daughter what the looking glass had revealed. "The Wizard has played a trick on us," she said. "Now I must break his spell."

Then she reached for her book of enchantments and spells. She discovered that the only way to break the Wizard's spell was to gain possession of a magic ring that he wore. But how was she to do this? She knew that he never took the ring from his finger.

Finally, she thought of a plan. She changed herself into a swallow and flew to the top of the Wizard's tower. Then, she slipped between the bars of the window and flew to the unhappy King.

"I am the Swan Fairy," she whispered, "and I have come to help you."

Tears of joy filled the young King's eyes. Then the Swan Fairy told him what the Wizard had done and what they must do to get the magic ring.

"You must convince Esmerelda to get the ring. It is the only way. You will have to be very nice to her when she visits you tomorrow."

The following morning, Esmerelda was overjoyed at how well the King received her. "Perhaps he is falling in love with me," she thought.

Harold told her of a dream that had come to him. In his dream, a fairy had told him that Princess Helena no longer wished to marry him. But the King would never be free to love anyone else, unless he wore the Wizard's ring for one day and one night.

Esmerelda was so happy at hearing these words that she ran off at once to find her father.

But when she told the story to the Wizard, he immediately became suspicious. Using his magic powers, he found out about the Swan Fairy's plan.

"I'll teach that meddling Swan Fairy," he said to himself. "I'll give her a ring all right. And when she touches this ring, she will turn into a marble statue."

He took a bright red ruby ring out of a drawer and placed it in a box. Esmerelda took it to the tower and gave it to Harold. Harold tossed the box to the Swan Fairy, who was in the courtyard below. As soon as she touched the ring, the Swan Fairy was turned into a marble statue!

Then the Wizard changed Harold into a blue parrot, and said, "You will fly through the forests until your beloved Helena strikes you down!"

Next, the Wizard went to the palace of the Swan Fairy. He seized Helena, took her into the deepest forest, and changed her into a tree.

"You will remain a tree until you strike down your beloved Harold," he said. Then he let out a great roar of laughter and disappeared in a puff of smoke.

As time went by, the blue parrot flew from forest to forest, always searching for Helena.

Then, one day he accidentally flew into the castle of a kindly Magician.

The Magician knew at once that this was an enchanted parrot. Perhaps he could break the spell.

He took the parrot into the forest, and went over to three tall trees that stood in a clearing. Then he began to chop around the roots of the trees, so that they would fall together.

The blue parrot remembered the words of the evil Wizard. One of the three trees might be his beloved Helena. He looked closely. The middle tree seemed to be the loveliest of the three. As the trees started to fall to the ground, the parrot swooped under the middle tree. Suddenly, there was a blinding flash. Where the parrot and the tree had been, Harold and Princess Helena stood hand in hand.

Breathlessly, Harold thanked the good Magician, and remembering the Swan Fairy, begged him to break the spell that was holding her captive in a marble statue.

"I will try," said the kindly Magician. And so he did.

He cast a magic spell over the wicked Wizard, who had grown fat and lazy and careless. By the next morning the Wizard was dead, and his evil spell was broken.

The marble statue turned back into the Swan Fairy. Harold and Helena were soon married, and reigned wisely and happily the rest of their days.

Esmerelda, who was really not a bad Princess—just not a pretty one—took over the kingdom of her father and became a good ruler. Sometime later she met and married a Prince who was not very handsome himself, and they lived happily ever after.